For my sister, Jackie - who taught me how to draw kites.

First published in 2009
by Hodder Children's Books
First published in paperback in 2010

Text and illustrations copyright © Michael Broad 2009

Hodder Children's Books
338 Euston Road
London NW1 3BH

Hodder Children's Books Australia
Level 17/207 Kent Street
Sydney NSW 2000

The right of Michael Broad to be identified as the author and the illustrator of this Work has been asserted by him in accordance with the Copyright, Designs and Patents Act 1988.

A catalogue record of this book is available from the British Library.

ISBN: 978 0 340 95695 3
10 9 8 7 6 5 4 3 2 1

Printed in China

Hodder Children's Books is a division of Hachette Children's Books.
An Hachette UK Company
www.hachette.co.uk

Can you spot the dung beetles?

Forget*Me*Not

MICHAEL BROAD

Hodder
Children's
Books

A division of Hachette Children's Books

AS THE HERD CROSSED THE PLAINS,
one little elephant was weary of walking.

'Mama, I'm bored,'
sighed Monty, dragging his
trunk along the dusty ground.

'The rains are coming soon,' said his mother.
'Then there'll be forget-me-nots.'

'What are forget-me-nots?'
asked Monty.

'Tiny blue flowers,' replied his mother.
'To help elephants to remember.'

'Remember what, Mama?' he asked.

'Remember to stay with the herd,'
she warned.

'Oh, I won't forget that,'
said Monty confidently.
'What else?'

'Never forget how much
I love you,' she smiled.

Later, Monty spied something strange beneath a tree and, forgetting his mother's warning, he stopped to investigate.

The little elephant sniffed and prodded and plucked the blue thing right out of the ground.

'A forget-me-not!' he gasped excitedly. 'I will take it straight to Mama.'

But when Monty looked around...

the herd was nowhere to be seen.

A flock of flamingos was gathered nearby so the little elephant hurried over. 'I found a forget-me-not, but forgot something important!' said Monty.

'You forgot to stay with the flock!' shrieked the flamingos.

'I don't think I belong to a flock,' Monty frowned.

'But the rains are coming!' they squawked,
'how will you shelter without a flock to huddle with?'

'I don't remember,' sighed Monty.

The young elephant walked on until he came upon a mob of meerkats. 'I found a forget-me-not, but forgot something important!' said Monty.

'You forgot to stay with the mob!' chuckled the meerkats.

'I don't think I belong to a mob,' Monty frowned.

'But the rains
are coming!'
they added,
'how will you
play without
a mob to look
out for you?'

'I don't
remember,'
sighed Monty.

As the sun began to set, the little elephant discovered
a colony of termites. 'I found a forget-me-not,
but forgot something important!' said Monty.

'You forgot
to stay with
the colony!'

gasped the termites.

'I don't think I belong to a colony,'
Monty frowned.

'But the rains are coming!'
they said, 'how will you build
a home without a colony?'

Monty couldn't remember and shed a tear on the dusty
ground. This was followed by another and another, until
there were too many tears to count.

The little elephant
looked up and saw
they were not
teardrops
at all, but
raindrops.

'The
rains
have
come!'

yelled the termites,
and disappeared inside
their mounds.

Monty was all alone as the rains came down,
but as the drops of water chimed upon the broken
bucket he recalled his mother's words.

'Never forget how much I love you,' she had said.

And Monty remembered
how Mama sheltered him.

And how she always
looked out for him.

And how the herd was his home.

Holding the memory close
to his heart, the brave little
elephant continued walking.

But it rained so hard Monty could not see where he was going. BUMP! He walked straight into a small group of trees.

'Shelter,' Monty thought and hid beneath them.
'I'll wait here till the rain stops.'

He thought he heard someone call his name, but it
must have been the wind whistling through the leaves above.

Then he heard it again. 'Monty!'

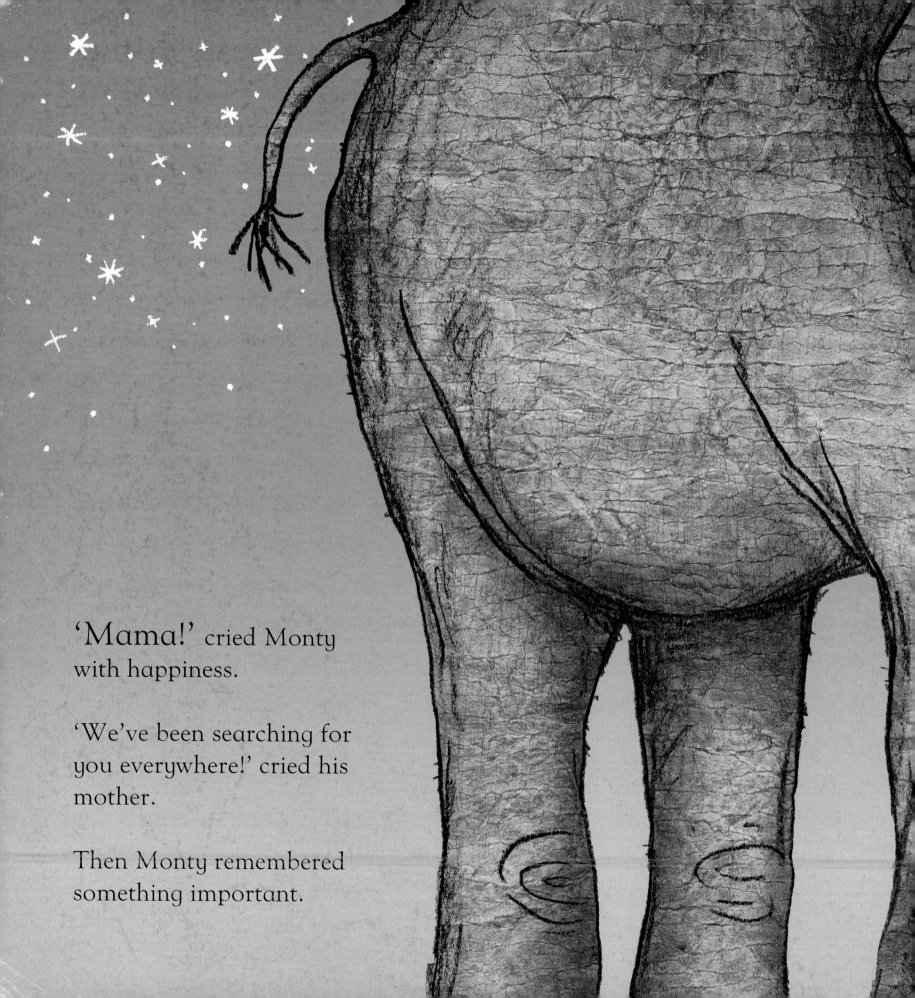

'Mama!' cried Monty
with happiness.

'We've been searching for
you everywhere!' cried his
mother.

Then Monty remembered
something important.

'I brought you a
forget-me-not, Mama,'
he yawned.

His mother took the
broken bucket and
placed it on her head.

'Thank you, Monty,'
she smiled. 'It's the prettiest
forget-me-not I've ever seen.'

When Monty awoke the next day, the plains were filled with tiny blue flowers! The little elephant leapt around, munching on the delicious forget-me-nots that help elephants to remember.

From that day on, Monty never forgot to stay with the herd,
or how much his Mama loved him.

And for ever after, he was always called
Forget*Me*Not.

Wish upon a forget-me-not
to remember to tell someone
special you love them.

Another wonderful
Forget*Me*Not
Adventure

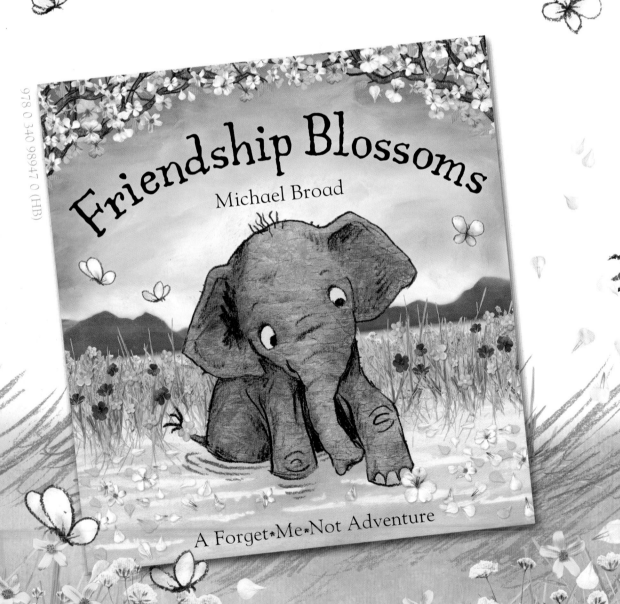

Friendship Blossoms

Michael Broad

A Forget*Me*Not Adventure

978 0 340 98947 0 (HB)